Karen's Doll Hospital

Look for these
and other books about Karen
in the
Baby-sitters Little Sister series:

Little Sister

Karen's Doll Hospital
Ann M. Martin

Illustrations by Susan Tang

A
LITTLE APPLE
PAPERBACK

SCHOLASTIC INC.
New York Toronto London Auckland Sydney

ISBN 0-590-45652-0

12 11 10 9 8 7 6 5 4 3 2 1   3 4 5 6 7 8/9

Printed in the U.S.A.   40

First Scholastic printing, February 1993

The author gratefully acknowledges
Stephanie Calmenson
for her help
with this book.

The Doll School

"*Oh, you beautiful doll! You great, big beautiful doll!*"

I was singing a song to my very best baby doll, Hyacynthia. When I was little Daddy used to sing that song to me. But I am not little anymore.

I am Karen Brewer. I am seven years old and in second grade. I have blonde hair and blue eyes. I wear pink glasses all the time, except when I am reading. When I am reading I wear blue glasses. And when I am sleeping, I do not wear any glasses at all.

1

I could not remember any more of the song, so I started over again from the beginning. *"Oh, you beautiful doll! You great, big . . ."*

"Pssst, Karen," whispered Nancy. "We know Hyacynthia is our most beautiful baby doll. But I think you are hurting the other dolls' feelings."

"I think Nancy is right," said Hannie.

Nancy, Hannie, and I were playing in Nancy's room. Nancy Dawes and Hannie Papadakis are my two best friends. We call ourselves the Three Musketeers.

"I know what. We can sing the song to everyone," I said. I started singing, *"Oh, you beautiful dolls! You great, big beautiful dolls!"*

Hannie and Nancy started singing, too. We sang the song three times. Very loudly. While we were singing, I was looking around the room.

Everywhere I turned, there were dolls, dolls, and more dolls! We had decided that very morning to bring all our dolls to Nancy's house for a party.

We had old dolls with tangled hair and smudgy faces. We had two rag dolls each. That made six rag dolls. (I am very good at math.) And we had about twenty Barbie dolls.

Our Doll Sisters were sitting together in the corner. The Doll Sisters are special. They are triplets. My Doll Sister is Terry. Hannie has Kerry. And Nancy has Merry. We earned the money to buy them all by ourselves.

And in a place of honor on Nancy's bed, there was Hyacynthia. My grandma and grandpa brought her back for me all the way from London, England. Hyacynthia is just perfect. She is the princess of dolls. I have to be gigundoly careful with her.

"You know what?" said Nancy. "I think we have enough dolls here to start a boarding school. It could be like the school in *The Secret Language*." (That is one of our favorite books.)

3

"Cool!" said Hannie. "I bet our dolls would love that."

I knew my dolls would love going to school. Especially Terry. I was a little worried about Hyacynthia. But boarding school was an opportunity too good to miss.

"It's a way cool idea!" I cried. I turned to Hyacynthia and said, "You will get to spend a little more time here at Nancy's house. And that will be fun, right?"

I could see from the look on Hyacynthia's face that she liked the idea just fine. Anyway, Nancy and I have joint custody of Hyacynthia. She spends part of the time at my house and part at Nancy's.

I think Hyacynthia likes it that way. Having two houses can be fun. That is something I know all about.

Grown-up Work

I will tell you why I know so much about living in two houses. That is because I have lived in two houses for a long time — the little house and the big house.

It wasn't always that way. I used to live only in the big house in Stoneybrook, Connecticut, with Mommy and Daddy and Andrew. (Andrew is my little brother. He is four going on five.) But then Mommy and Daddy started having troubles. Not with Andrew and me. But with each other. They were fighting a *lot*. Their troubles got so bad, they decided to get a divorce.

Daddy stayed in the big house. That is the house he grew up in. Mommy, Andrew, and I moved to a little house not too far away.

Mommy and Daddy each got married again to other people. Mommy married Seth Engle. That makes him my stepfather. He came to live at the little house. So now there are Mommy, Seth, Andrew, me, Rocky (Seth's cat), Midgie (Seth's dog), and Emily Junior (my pet rat).

Daddy married Elizabeth Thomas. That makes her my stepmother. She was married once before and had four kids. So here are the people who live at the big house: Daddy, Elizabeth, David Michael (he's seven, like me), Sam and Charlie (they're so grown-up, they're in high school), and Kristy. (She's thirteen and pretty grown-up, too. She is also the best big stepsister ever!)

There is one more kid at the big house.

That's Emily Michelle. Daddy and Elizabeth adopted her from a faraway country called Vietnam. She is two and a half and really cute. (I named my pet rat after her.)

And there is one more grown-up. That's Nannie. She is Elizabeth's mother. She helps take care of everyone at the big house, especially Emily Michelle.

There are lots of pets at the big house, too. There is Boo-Boo (Daddy's cranky old cat), Shannon (David Michael's big, goofy puppy), Crystal Light the Second (my goldfish), and Goldfishie (Andrew's you-know-whatie).

Andrew and I live at the little house most of the time. But we live at the big house at least every other weekend and on some holidays, plus two weeks in the summer.

I will tell you something. Living at two houses is not always easy. One thing that helps is having two of lots of different things. That way Andrew and I do not have to carry so much back and forth. For instance, I have two stuffed cats — Moosie at the big house, and Goosie at the little house. I have two pairs of sneakers. I have two bicycles. I even have two pieces of Tickly, my special blanket. That is because I used to leave Tickly behind at one house or the other, and then I would get upset. Finally, I tore Tickly in two so I could have a piece at each house.

And you already know that I have two best friends. Nancy lives next door to Mommy's house. Hannie lives across the street and one house over from Daddy's.

I have special names for Andrew and me. Since we have two of so many things, I call us Karen Two-Two and Andrew Two-Two. I got the idea from a book my teacher, Ms. Colman, read to us. It was called *Jacob Two-Two Meets the Hooded Fang*.

Hmm. I wonder if calling us Two-Twos is babyish. No. I don't think so. But if it is, I hope someone will tell me. I do not want to be babyish. I want to be grown-up, like

Sam and Charlie and Kristy. You should see the homework they get. It is grown-up work. That's what I want. Grown-up work, just like theirs. No more baby work for me!

The Bad News

"Attention, all dolls!" I called. "Use your indoor voices, please. It is much too noisy."

Grown-ups are always telling me to use my indoor voice. So that was rule number one at the Three Musketeers Boarding School.

Running a boarding school was gigundoly hard work. It took a lot of time. (I asked Mommy if I could move into Nancy's house, but she said no. Boo.)

On Saturday, our dolls were having a pretend food fight. "Girls, stop throwing food!" cried Nancy. "Oh, look. You hit Hyacynthia. There is chocolate pudding all over her beautiful blue dress."

"I do not think the girls in *The Secret Language* behaved so badly," said Hannie with a sigh. "I wonder what we are doing wrong."

"Well, they had that mean old housemother. And we do not want to be mean. We want to be nice. Just like Ms. Colman," I said.

I looked at Terry, my very own Doll Sister. She did not look happy. I think she was upset because she could not sleep in a room with her sisters, Merry and Kerry.

"There are only two beds in each room," I explained. "If you are still unhappy next week we will let you have a turn with one of your sisters. But your roommate, Jasmine, is very nice. Try your best to get along."

I wanted to be grown-up and fair. But I knew I would not be happy either if Nancy and Hannie shared a room and I was left out.

"Recess!" called Hannie. "Who wants to play statues?"

All the dolls wanted to play. Nancy, Hannie, and I were the sculptors. We put our dolls in beautiful poses. Then we were supposed to pick a winner. But we couldn't.

"Everyone wins!" I said.

"I will get Mommy's camera," said Nancy. "We should take pictures for the Three Musketeers Boarding School yearbook."

Nancy ran out of the room. When she came back, she said, "Karen, your mommy called. She asked you to come home. She wants you to run errands with her."

"Do you think you will be okay without me?" I asked. "I will only be gone a little while."

"We'll be fine," said Hannie. "But come back soon. The girls need you for their math lesson this afternoon."

"Okay!" I called. "See you later!" I

gave Hyacynthia a special smile before I left. I hoped the other dolls did not see.

I was sorry to leave Nancy's house. But I knew the dolls would be fine. They were in very good hands.

Mommy took Andrew and me to the mall for new sneakers. We each got two pairs. That is because we are Two-Twos.

When we got back to the house, the phone was ringing and ringing. Mommy answered it. "It's for you, Karen. It's Nancy," she said.

"Hi!" I said into the phone. "What's up?"

"Could you come over right away?" said Nancy. "We have some bad news."

The Accident

I did not run to Nancy's house. I *flew*. Nancy was waiting downstairs for me. She was holding the door open. I raced inside and up the stairs.

The bad news was laid out right on Nancy's dresser. It was my dear, beautiful baby doll, Hyacynthia. One of her china legs had been smashed to pieces. And her poor face. Hyacynthia used to have two smooth, rosy cheeks. Now one cheek was chipped. And it was not rosy anymore.

I went to the dresser and cradled my baby doll in my arms.

"There, there, Hyacynthia," I whispered softly. I turned to Nancy and Hannie. "What happened?" I asked.

"Well, after you left we decided to let the dolls have free play," said Nancy. "Hyacynthia wanted to go on a swing."

"So we made one for her out of an old baby blanket," said Hannie. "I put her in the swing really carefully."

"You did not!" hissed Nancy. "You let go too fast! You dropped her!"

"No, I didn't!" shouted Hannie. "You started swinging too fast. *You* dropped her!"

"I did not!" cried Nancy.

"You did too!" cried Hannie.

"Did not!" said Nancy.

"Did too!" said Hannie.

"Stop yelling," I said. "You are upsetting Hyacynthia."

"I'm sorry," said Nancy. "I'm sorry Hyacynthia got hurt."

16

"We never meant to hurt her," said Hannie.

"I know you would not hurt her on purpose," I said. "I know you both love her a lot."

"I'll help you pay to fix her," said Hannie.

"Me, too," said Nancy.

"Thanks," I said.

All of a sudden, I started to worry. When I got Hyacynthia, Mommy and Seth made me promise I would be extra careful with her. That is because she's such an expensive doll.

I knew Mommy and Seth would be unhappy. But I had to tell them what had happened. I decided to get it over with right away.

"Maybe it is time for my dolls to leave school," I said. "Um, I think summer vacation is here."

I felt a couple of tears roll down my cheek. I hoped Hannie and Nancy did not see me. They felt bad enough already.

I gathered my dolls together.

"Here. You can put them in this," said Nancy. She gave me a pillowcase.

I put all my dolls inside. Except for Hyacynthia. I wrapped her up carefully in the baby blanket.

Another tear rolled down my cheek. This time Hannie and Nancy saw it.

"We really are sorry, Karen," they said.

I nodded to let them know I wasn't mad. I really wasn't. I was sad. And worried. And confused. I turned and left the room. By the time I got downstairs, Nancy and Hannie were arguing again.

"You should have held on to Hyacynthia," said Nancy.

"You should not have started swinging her so fast," said Hannie. "It's your fault she broke."

"It is not!" said Nancy.

"Is too!" said Hannie.

"Is not!" said Nancy.

They were still arguing when I closed the door behind me.

The Doll Hospital

I slipped into my house and tiptoed up the stairs.

"Karen? Is that you?" called Mommy from the kitchen. "Are you okay?"

"I'm okay," I called back. But Hyacynthia is not, I thought.

I put my dolls down on my bed. I decided to tell Goosie what had happened first. For practice.

"Hyacynthia has been in a terrible accident," I told Goosie. "She needs a lot of loving."

20

Goosie gave Hyacynthia a kiss and a hug. I could tell that Hyacynthia felt a whole lot better.

I covered her up again in the baby blanket. I did not want Mommy and Seth to see what had happened. Not right away. I wanted to break the news to them slowly.

"Let's go, Hyacynthia," I said. "I hope they will not be too, too mad at me."

Mommy and Seth were sitting in the kitchen. They were drinking coffee.

"Hi, Karen," said Seth. "Do you want to talk to us about something? You look upset."

"I have bad news," I said bravely. "Hyacynthia has been in an accident. I am really sorry. I know I promised to be careful with her. But . . . but . . ."

I uncovered Hyacynthia so they could see what had happened.

Mommy and Seth looked at each other. It was not an angry look. It was a sad look.

"I am sorry your doll is hurt, honey," Mommy said.

"These things happen," said Seth. He gently stroked Hyacynthia's head.

"It wasn't my fault," I explained. "Nancy and Hannie were just playing with her. They always try to be careful. This really was an accident."

"Let's see how badly she is hurt," said Seth. He took Hyacynthia from my arms.

"Hmm. Her face is chipped. And the bottom half of her right leg is gone," said Seth.

I felt my eyes filling up again.

"I am sure Hyacynthia can be repaired," said Mommy.

Seth got the Yellow Pages from the closet. He started flipping through the book.

"Here we go. Here is a place called Mr. Kelly's Toy Repair. It is right here in Stoneybrook," he said.

"I don't remember seeing a toy repair shop downtown," said Mommy.

"It isn't downtown. In fact, it is not near any stores at all. It is on Reade Street. I don't even know where that is," said Seth.

"Let's call and find out about it," said Mommy.

Seth called the number that was listed in the book.

"We have a doll here that needs mending," he said. He described Hyacynthia's injuries. (Poor Hyacynthia!)

"Do you think you can fix her?" asked Seth. "We could bring her over right away."

I jumped up from my chair. I wanted to leave that very minute. Then I heard Seth say, "Oh, you're closing now. Well, Monday will be fine then. Thank you." He hung up the phone.

"Monday? We have to wait until Monday?" I asked. "Did he sound nice? Can he fix Hyacynthia?"

"Mr. Kelly sounded like a very nice, elderly man," said Seth. "He thinks he can fix Hyacynthia. He said to bring her in on Monday."

"Okay, but I want to go, too," I said.

Hyacynthia would be scared without me."

"I will take you there after school," said Mommy.

I cradled Hyacynthia in my arms. "You are going to the doll hospital on Monday. So do not worry. You'll be okay. I just know it."

May Day

"Guess what?" I said. "Hyacynthia has to go to the hospital. I am taking her there later."

It was Monday morning. I was at school. I was talking to my two best friends. But Hannie and Nancy were not talking much.

"Is it the same hospital I went to?" asked Nancy. (Nancy went to the hospital once to have her appendix taken out.)

"No. She is going to the doll hospital," I replied. "Her doctor is Mr. Kelly. He will try to fix her."

"I hope he can do it," said Hannie. "She would not be going to the hospital at all if certain people had not swung her so fast."

"You mean if certain people had not let go of her so fast," said Nancy.

Uh-oh. Hannie and Nancy were fighting again. I was glad when Ms. Colman came into the room.

"See you later," I said.

I hurried to my desk in the front row. I used to sit in the back with Hannie and Nancy. Then I got glasses and Ms. Colman moved me up front so I could see better. Now I sit next to Natalie Springer and Ricky Torres. (Ricky is my pretend husband. We got married on the playground one day.) Natalie and Ricky wear glasses, too. So does Ms. Colman.

After attendance, Ms. Colman said, "I have a new assignment for you. I think you will find it interesting."

I sat up tall. I love new assignments! One time our assignment was to make clay animals. Then we went to the zoo and saw our animals on display in the visitor's room.

"I would like you to do a research project," said Ms. Colman.

Research! That sounded like grown-up work to me. It sounded like the kind of grown-up work Sam and Charlie and Kristy did.

Research. I wrote the word in big letters in my notebook. I wanted to do a gigundoly good job. I wanted to get an A. No, an A+! No, an A + + +!

Ms. Colman was still talking. I decided to listen carefully. It was the grown-up thing to do.

"Each of you will work with a partner. You are to find out about a holiday that is not already familiar to you," continued Ms. Colman. "You will write a brief report and make a presentation to the class. The presentation may be in any form — a skit, or an art project, for example. Are there any questions?"

I could not think of a grown-up question,

so I didn't ask anything at all.

"All right, then, I will assign partners and you may choose a holiday to work on," said Ms. Colman.

Ms. Colman assigned me to Natalie. Natalie's socks droop all the time. And she is pretty clumsy. But I like Natalie. I decided we would have fun together.

I turned to a clean page in my notebook and took out my best, sharpest pencil. I asked Natalie (nicely) to please pull up her socks.

"We have got to do everything right," I explained.

"I have a question," said Natalie. "How can we pick a holiday we do not know about?"

"I have an idea. We will ask Ms. Colman if we can look at her calendar. We will find a holiday there," I said.

Ms. Colman told me that was a very good way to begin our research.

We started at January and turned the pages. We passed Groundhog Day and Val-

entine's Day. We passed April Fool's Day
and Easter and Passover.

"Here is a holiday I don't know about,"
I said. I was pointing to May Day.

"I do not know about that holiday
either," said Natalie.

We decided to research May Day. By the
time we finished, we would know everything there was to know.

Mr. Kelly

"Hi, Mommy! Hi, Andrew! Hi, Hyacynthia!" I called when I saw Mommy's car pull up at school.

"Hi, honey," said Mommy. "Are you ready to go to Mr. Kelly's?"

"I'm ready," I said. I climbed into the back seat with Andrew and Hyacynthia. Hyacynthia was in a basket. A blanket was wrapped around her. I had given her a bag with three oatmeal raisin cookies, and a tiny book of poems. I had made sure she was all ready for her trip, even before I went to school.

"The address is six-oh-six Reade Street," said Mommy. "Everyone, please buckle up."

First we drove past our house. Andrew and I waved. Then we turned right on one street. Left on another. Right. Left. I felt as if we were going in circles.

"Are you sure you know the way, Mommy?" I asked.

"We are almost there," Mommy replied.

Soon we were in a neighborhood with dark old houses and great big trees. I hoped Mr. Kelly did not live here.

"Ooh. Spooky," said Andrew.

"Shhh!" I whispered. "You'll scare Hyacynthia."

I wondered if Morbidda Destiny's relatives lived here. (She is the witch who lives next door to Daddy's house.) If anyone who looked like Morbidda Destiny answered Mr. Kelly's door, I was leaving.

"Here we are," said Mommy. "Six-oh-six Reade Street."

We stopped in front of a big, gray house. It looked like a perfect house for a mystery. A monster mystery! If a monster answered the door, I was leaving.

I hugged Hyacynthia close to me as we walked up the steps. Andrew hung on to the back of Mommy's coat while she rang the bell.

Ding-ing-ing-ing. Dong-ong-ong-ong. (Ooh, creepy.) I took a step back. We waited and waited. Then the door creaked open.

A man with bright white hair, round wire glasses, and a big smile peered out. He said, "I am Mr. Kelly. What a pretty doll you have there!"

I liked Mr. Kelly right away. I already had plenty of grandfathers. But if I needed a new one, Mr. Kelly would be perfect.

"Hi!" I said, stepping up to the door. "I am Karen Brewer. And this is Hyacynthia."

33

After everyone said hello, Mr. Kelly took us inside. Nobody else was in the house. I guessed Mr. Kelly lived by himself.

He led us to a big room upstairs.

"This is the toy repair room where I do most of my work," he said.

"Oh, boy!" cried Andrew. There were toys everywhere.

We walked through the toy room to another, smaller room. "This is where Hyacynthia will stay," said Mr. Kelly. "This room is just for dolls."

"It really is a doll hospital," I said.

Mr. Kelly lifted Hyacynthia out of her basket and examined her carefully.

"Yes, I am sure I can fix her. I will replace her leg and repaint her face. But you will have to leave her with me, maybe for a few weeks," said Mr. Kelly.

"Is that all right with you, Karen?" asked Mommy.

I hated to leave Hyacynthia. But I knew I had to.

"Okay," I said.

34

"You can call me any time you feel worried," said Mr. Kelly.

"Really?" I asked.

"Really," Mr. Kelly replied.

I kissed Hyacynthia's chipped cheek. "Don't you worry," I said. "I am leaving you in very good hands."

The Toy Man

It was a big-house weekend. Mommy dropped Andrew and me off at Daddy's just before dinnertime.

"How is Hyacynthia feeling?" asked Daddy.

"Mr. Kelly said she was fine, but that was at three-thirty," I replied. "I will go call him again!"

"Whoa, young lady. One call a day is plenty," said Daddy. "But I can take you to see her tomorrow."

"All right!" I cried. I could hardly wait.

Daddy said he knew Mr. Kelly when he was a boy. He said the kids called Mr. Kelly "The Toy Man." Mr. Kelly even fixed Daddy's fire truck once.

After dinner, I made three different get-well cards for Hyacynthia. Then I cut a heart out of red felt, and wrote *I Love You* on it with glitter.

The next morning, I called Mr. Kelly. He said to come over any time. Daddy drove me over right after breakfast.

Ding-ing-ing-ing. Dong-ong-ong-ong. Mr. Kelly's bell did not scare me anymore. But we still had to wait and wait. That is because Mr. Kelly is old. It takes him a long time to go up and down stairs.

"Hi, Mr. Kelly!" I said when he opened the door.

"Welcome," said Mr. Kelly. "Hyacynthia has been looking forward to your visit. And so have I."

Daddy introduced himself and thanked Mr. Kelly for fixing his fire truck when he was a boy.

When we got upstairs, Daddy stopped in the toy repair room. I went to the doll hospital with Mr. Kelly.

"Hyacynthia! I have missed you so much!" I cried.

The bottom half of Hyacynthia's leg was still missing. But her right cheek was bright and rosy again. She looked very happy to see me.

I gave her the cards and the heart I made. Then we all sat down by the window to visit.

"Daddy says when he was little, the kids called you 'The Toy Man,'" I said.

"Yes, they did. I was very proud of that name," said Mr. Kelly. "You see, when *I* was a boy, I grew up in a country called Ireland. A war was going on there. That is something I hope you will never know about. Toys were hard to come by. The few toys I had were left behind when my family moved to safety."

"That is very sad," I said. "I would

never, ever want to leave Hyacynthia, or Moosie, or Goosie, or Terry."

"Toys are important to children. That is why, when I came to America, I started to fix toys. Now I mostly fix the toys no one wants anymore. I make them look like new so I can give them to needy children at Christmas," said Mr. Kelly.

"You're just like Santa Claus!" I said.

"If I could be anyone else, anyone at all, Santa Claus is who I would want to be," said Mr. Kelly.

All of a sudden I noticed a twinkle in Mr. Kelly's eye. For a minute I thought maybe he *was* Santa Claus.

We talked until Daddy said it was time to go.

"You are welcome here as often as you like, Karen," said Mr. Kelly.

"Thank you," I said. "I will be back very soon."

I gave Hyacynthia a kiss on her shiny, new cheek. I gave Mr. Kelly a kiss on his cheek, too.

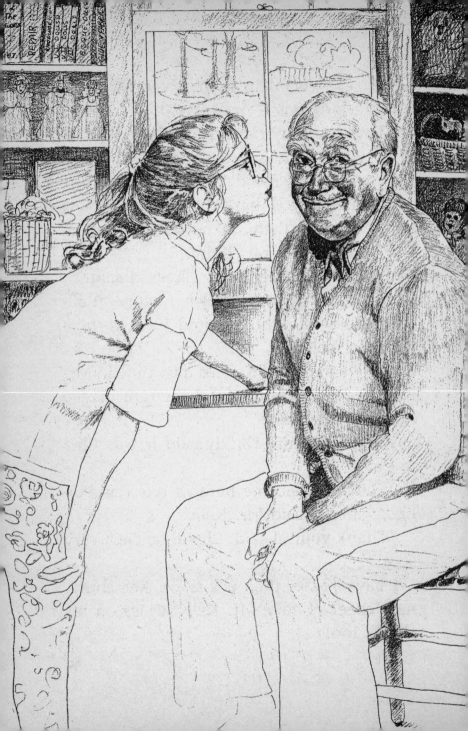

When I got home I called Hannie and Nancy. I told them about my visit. They were so glad that Hyacynthia was going to live. They forgot all about fighting.

I was gigundoly happy. Hyacynthia was getting well. And Nancy and Hannie were friends again.

Natalie's Maypole

"I think we picked the coolest holiday," I said to Natalie.

We were at the little house working on our research project. We had just finished a very grown-up snack of cheese and crackers and olives. (The olives were my idea. I asked for coffee, too. But Mommy said no.)

"Do you girls need any help with your work this afternoon?" asked Mommy.

"I don't think so," I replied. "We want to do this project all by ourselves."

"Well, just call if you need me," Mommy said.

"Thank you, Mrs. Engle," said Natalie.

"Yes, thank you, Mrs. Engle," I said in my most grown-up voice.

After school, Natalie and I had done a lot of important research at the library. We had borrowed three books on holidays. And we had copied the page about May Day from the encyclopedia.

I picked up one of the books and began to read out loud to Natalie. "May Day (May first) is a celebration of spring. Some people think that May Day celebrations began in ancient Egypt and India."

"I want a turn to read," said Natalie.

"Okay," I said. "You read and I will take notes for our report."

Natalie continued reading where I had left off. "Children often gather spring flowers. They make May baskets and have May Day parties. People gather in villages to dance around a Maypole and sing May Day songs."

Natalie looked up. "Did you get all that?"

"Flowers. Baskets. Parties. Maypole. Dancing. Singing. That's it!" I replied.

"Ka-ren!" said Natalie. "Those are not good notes."

"I got the important parts," I told her. "Does it say what a Maypole is?"

"Umm . . . It says here that a Maypole is a pole with brightly colored ribbons hanging down from the top. People dance around the Maypole while holding the ribbons. As they dance, the ribbons get wrapped around the pole."

"Is there a picture?" I asked.

"I don't see one," replied Natalie.

"We will have to do more research," I said. "Can you go to the library with me again tomorrow?"

"Sure," said Natalie. "And when we find out what a Maypole is, I could make one for us. A real one. I am very good at arts and crafts."

"I will write the report. I am very good at spelling. And I will use my best hand-

writing," I said. "This will be the most grown-up research project in the history of second grade!"

"I hope I don't have to buy too many things for the Maypole," said Natalie.

"I will help you pay for them," I said. "But we have to use our own money. That is the grown-up thing to do."

"This is so much fun!" said Natalie. "I'm glad you're my partner, Karen."

"I'm glad you're my partner, too," I said. And I really did mean it.

The Good-as-New Doll

Ring! Ring! It was Tuesday night at the little house.

"Karen, it's for you," said Seth. "It's Mr. Kelly."

"Mr. Kelly!" I cried.

I had visited Mr. Kelly three more times since the day I went there with Daddy. And I had called him every day. But he had never called *me* before. Maybe . . . just maybe . . .

"Hello, Mr. Kelly," I said. "How are you?

How is Hyacynthia? Is she ready to come home?"

Mr. Kelly said Hyacynthia was ready. Yes!

I asked Mommy if we could get her the next day. And I asked her if Nancy and Hannie could come with us. Mommy said yes to both things.

"See you tomorrow!" I said to Mr. Kelly.

I called Nancy right away. Her mommy said she could come with us. "I hope Hyacynthia recognizes me," said Nancy.

Then I called Hannie. She could come, too. "I cannot wait to meet Mr. Kelly," she said.

The next day after school, the Three Musketeers piled into Mommy's car. We reached Mr. Kelly's house in no time at all.

"Mr. Kelly, these are my two best friends, the ones I told you about," I said proudly. "This is Nancy Dawes. And this is Hannie Papadakis."

"I am honored to have a visit from the

Three Musketeers," said Mr. Kelly.

I wanted to go to the doll hospital to see Hyacynthia. But first I had to give Hannie and Nancy the grand tour.

"This is the repair shop where Mr. Kelly fixes all the toys," I said. "Do you see how many toys there are? After they have been fixed up, Mr. Kelly gives them to needy children at Christmas."

I could see that Nancy and Hannie were impressed.

"Here are Mr. Kelly's tools," I said, opening a cupboard door. I knew *everything* about Mr. Kelly's Toy Repair Shop.

"And now I will take you to the doll hospital," I said. "Please try to keep your voices down. Some of the dolls are very ill. They need their rest."

I led the way to the small room where the dolls were kept. Hyacynthia was not in her usual spot.

"Where is Hyacynthia?" I asked Mr. Kelly.

Mr. Kelly pointed to a bench.

"She is with the good-as-new dolls," he explained.

We hurried over to Hyacynthia.

"She looks perfect!" said Nancy.

"She looks like she was never hurt at all!" said Hannie.

I hugged Hyacynthia to me. "I am so happy you are all better," I said. "I hope you said thank you to Mr. Kelly."

Hannie and Nancy paid for the repairs just as they promised. While they were paying, I whispered something important in Mommy's ear. Mommy nodded. I turned to Mr. Kelly.

"Mr. Kelly," I said. "Would you like to come to the little house for dinner on Friday?"

"I would love to, Karen. Thank you for asking," Mr. Kelly replied.

I left Mr. Kelly's Toy Repair shop with Mommy, my two best friends, and my good-as-new doll cradled in my arms.

Karen's Doll Hospital

"We're back!" I announced to Goosie and Terry and all of Hyacynthia's friends.

My room looked gigundoly beautiful. I had decorated it the night before when I found out that Hyacynthia was coming home. There were streamers (left over from Andrew's birthday party). And I had made a big banner that said: WELCOME HOME, HYACYNTHIA!

"Now don't everyone crowd around at once," I warned. "Hyacynthia is still recovering. She needs her rest."

"Mommy says when someone's been sick, they need three R's," said Hannie.

"Reading, 'riting, and 'rithmetic?" asked Nancy.

"No," said Hannie. "Rest, relaxation, and um . . . um . . ."

"Raisins!" I exclaimed. That sounded like good food for a recovering patient.

I gave Hyacynthia some make-believe raisins. Then we tucked her into her cradle.

"Go to sleep now, Hyacynthia," said Nancy. "You've had a long day."

"Psst," I whispered. (I did not want to disturb Hyacynthia.) "Let's go get the dolls from boarding school and bring them here. They can keep Hyacynthia company while she is getting well."

"Good idea," whispered Nancy.

We tiptoed out of the room. I told Mommy we were going over to Nancy's house.

Nancy's and Hannie's dolls were having a study period.

"Your former classmate, Hyacynthia, has

been ill," Hannie told them. "Who would like to visit her?"

All the dolls wanted to go. We filled up three pillowcases with dolls and stuffed animals, too. We brought them back to my room.

"Make yourselves at home," I said. "I am sure Hyacynthia will be glad to see you when she wakes up."

"Oh, look," said Hannie. "My Doll Sister has a scratch on her cheek."

"Poor Kerry," said Nancy. "I hope Pokey didn't scratch her." (Pokey is Nancy's kitten.)

I ran to the bathroom and got a Band-Aid to put on Kerry's cheek.

"This is perfect," I said. "We can open a doll hospital here while Hyacynthia is getting better. She will have lots of company. We can pretend we are doll doctors."

"And animal doctors," added Hannie.

"We can use shoe boxes for beds," I suggested. "Mommy and Seth have lots of those."

"We have to make separate wards for dolls who have something catchy," said Hannie.

"You are right," I said. "I just heard a doll sneezing over in the corner. That will be the catchy ward."

Mommy gave me lots of shoe boxes. And she let me have a thermometer and two empty aspirin bottles to put on the shelves. By the time we were finished my room looked like a real doll hospital.

"It is time to make our rounds," I said.

We looked in on Hyacynthia, our sickest patient, first. She was recovering very nicely, thank you.

The First Patient

On Thursday, Ms. Colman made an important announcement about our research projects.

"I would like you to begin sharing your projects next week. The written reports will be due on Thursday. Your presentations will be made on Friday," said Ms. Colman. "Will any of you have trouble being ready then?"

I shook my head hard so Ms. Colman could see I would have no trouble at all.

"I will give you some time now to work

with your partners," said Ms. Colman. "I am here to help if you need me."

I pushed my chair over to Natalie's desk so I was sitting right beside her. Natalie pulled up her socks. We were ready to begin.

"I am almost finished with our report," I said. "I am writing it so, so neatly. That is why it is taking me a long time."

"I bought all the things for the Maypole," said Natalie. "I got a really tall broomstick. The broom part twists right off. And I got ribbons, and gold foil. We can make gold balls just like the ones we saw in the picture."

"Are the ribbons different colors?" I asked.

"Every color in the rainbow," said Natalie.

"Here is what I think we should do for our presentation," I said. "I will say a few things about our holiday. You can say a few things about Maypoles."

"Then we can do the Maypole dance,"

said Natalie. "Should we ask some of the other kids to do it with us?"

"I bet Hannie and Nancy would help. But I do not think Pamela or Leslie or Jannie would," I said. (Pamela Harding is my sometimes enemy. Leslie Morris and Jannie Gilbert are her friends.)

"How about Ricky and Bobby?" asked Natalie.

"They will hate the idea. But let's ask them anyway. Maybe Ricky will say yes because he is my husband," I said.

"And if Ricky says yes, then Bobby will, too," said Natalie.

We did not have any more to say about our project, so I told Natalie about the doll hospital.

"My best baby doll, Hyacynthia, was in an accident," I said.

"Oh, I'm sorry," said Natalie.

"Thank you. She is much better now. But she still needs to recover. She is in the doll hospital in my room," I explained.

"That is very, very interesting," said Natalie. "You see, I have a doll who should probably be in the hospital, too. Her arm snapped off just last night."

"Oh, no!" I said.

"Oh, yes," said Natalie. "The box she came in says her arm can be snapped on again. But I do not know about that. It looks pretty serious to me."

"I think you should bring her to school tomorrow. I will take a look at her. If she needs to go to the hospital I can take her home with me," I said.

"What a relief!" said Natalie. "I have been worried about her all day."

How exciting! A patient. My first real patient. Dr. Karen Brewer, doll specialist, to the rescue!

Pudding

It was Friday. Ms. Colman was already taking attendance when Natalie came in.

"Did . . . you . . . bring . . . her?" I asked. We are not supposed to talk during attendance. So I did not make any noise. I just mouthed the words.

"What?" asked Natalie. Only she said it out loud.

"Please take your seat quietly," said Ms. Colman.

I could see yellow hair poking out of

Natalie's knapsack. Hurray! My very first patient.

During recess Natalie introduced us.

"This is Pudding," said Natalie. She started digging into her bag. "And here's her arm," she said.

I shook the arm's hand.

"That is not funny," said Natalie. "If you are going be funny, I will not give Pudding to you."

"I'm sorry," I said. "I promise to take good care of her. My hospital has an excellent reputation, you know. I have not lost a patient yet."

"You have to promise not to fool around with her hair," said Natalie.

"Why?" I asked.

"Pudding is a special Baby Grow-My-Hair Doll. When you pull her hair it gets longer. But you can't make it shorter again. And I do not want her hair to be long yet."

"I promise I will not touch her hair," I

said, even though it looked like it could use a good brushing.

I checked Pudding into the hospital right after school.

"We have a new patient," I announced. "Her arm broke off. I am going to have to operate to put it back."

I let Goosie be the nurse. He held Pudding's arm until I was ready. I tied a handkerchief around my face. An important surgeon must always wear a mask.

I took Pudding's arm from Goosie. Snap! It popped right back into place. I sat Pudding up on my bed.

"Now you must rest," I told my patient.

I made a bed for Pudding next to Hyacynthia. I thought they would get along well.

Before I tended to my other patients, I changed my clothes. It was a special night. Mr. Kelly, my good friend, was coming for dinner.

Achoo! Someone in the catchy ward sneezed.

62

"Was that you, Terry?" I asked. I took Terry's temperature. (She had a slight fever.) Then I changed Kerry's bandage. (Her scratch was almost healed.)

The phone started ringing in the next room. I could hear Mommy talking.

"I am so sorry. Thank you for calling to let us know. Please tell him we hope he will feel better soon," she said.

Mommy came into my room and sat down on my bed.

"Honey, Mr. Kelly's neighbor called. He wanted to let us know that Mr. Kelly had a mild heart attack yesterday. He is in the hospital."

My eyes started filling up the way they did when Hyacynthia had her accident.

"I don't want Mr. Kelly to be in the hospital," I moaned.

Mommy put her arms around me. "I know you are sad. But I do not think we have to be too worried. The heart attack was very mild. He should be home in a few days."

That made me feel a little better.

"I am going to make Mr. Kelly a get-well card. Will you take it to him for me?" I asked. (I knew children were not allowed to visit in the hospital.)

"That would be very nice," said Mommy.

"And will you take him some dolls to keep him company?" I asked. "They can all get well together."

Mommy promised she would go the very next day.

I got to work on my card. It said: *Get Well Soon. Love, Karen, Hyacynthia, Goosie, Terry, Merry, Kerry . . .*

I kept writing names until the card was filled up.

Pudding's Problem Hair

After dinner, Dr. Brewer, Dr. Dawes, and Dr. Papadakis were making rounds at the doll hospital. (Mommy let me invite Nancy and Hannie to dinner since Mr. Kelly could not come.)

"I am glad that Jasmine was wearing her bicycle helmet," said Nancy. "Or she might not have survived!"

"And I am happy to report that Ruby will walk again," said Hannie.

Hannie finished tying a Popsicle stick cast

on her doll. Jasmine and Ruby had been in a very bad bicycle crash.

Meantime, I was patching up one of our rag doll's knees. It was torn and I had to sew it.

"It looks like this patient is going to have a small scar," I announced. "I had to use red thread because Mommy didn't have any pink."

I finished the last three big stitches. Then we moved on to our next patient.

"This is Pudding," I said. "Her mother is Natalie Springer. You could probably tell from her droopy socks."

I pulled up Pudding's socks for her.

"When Pudding came into the hospital her arm was broken off. As you can see, I was able to put it back on with no trouble," I reported.

"I am keeping her for observation till to-morrow," I said. "Then Natalie is coming to pick her up."

We continued working for a couple more

hours. There were a lot of sick patients who needed us. When the last one had been washed and sewn and bandaged, I looked in on our newest patient, Pudding, one more time.

"You know what Pudding's real problem is," I announced. "She has problem hair."

I pulled a few of Pudding's blonde coils out of her special Grow-My-Hair head. (I had wanted to do that ever since Natalie told me how it worked.)

"You better not touch her hair," said Nancy.

"You are right," I said. "I promised Natalie I would leave it alone."

"Hannie," said Mommy. She was standing at the door. "Your daddy is in the car. It's time to go home."

"I guess it's time for me to go, too," said Nancy. "Will you watch my patients for me?"

"Do not worry about a thing. I will call you if there are any emergencies," I replied.

68

When Hannie and Nancy were gone, I picked up Pudding again. If I make her hair grow just a little, Natalie won't even notice, I thought.

I gathered Pudding's hair into a ponytail and pulled.

Yikes. I must have pulled too hard. Suddenly I was holding all of Pudding's hair in my hand. Pudding was completely bald!

I tried to squeeze the hair back into the tiny holes in Pudding's head. But it would not go. Oops. Natalie was not going to be happy.

I tied a scarf on Pudding's head. I did not want to look at what I had done.

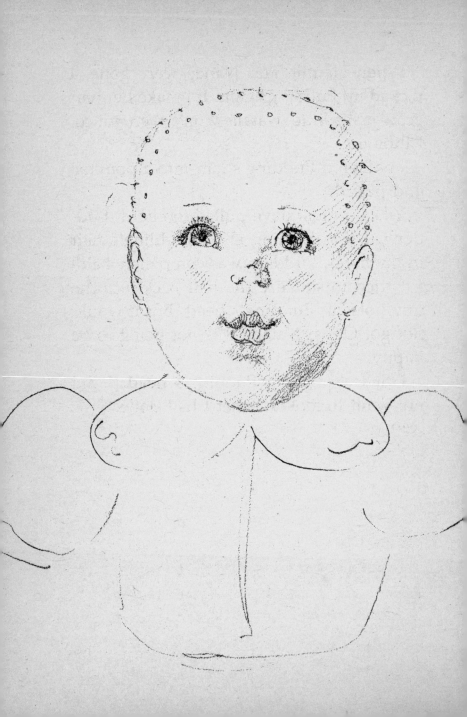

Where Is Pudding?

"I'd better go now," said Mommy.

It was ten-thirty on Saturday morning. Mommy was going to visit Mr. Kelly.

"Do you have his get-well bag?" I asked.

"It's in the car," Mommy replied. "I am sure Mr. Kelly will love it."

In the bag was the card I made, a picture of the Three Musketeers that Daddy had taken, and my very favorite stuffed animals and dolls. Hyacynthia was still too weak to travel. But I was sending the Doll

Sisters: Terry, Merry, and Kerry. And some others.

When Mommy left, Andrew asked, "Want to play catch?"

"Okay," I said. I knew I should be working on my research project. Natalie was coming over at noon. We were supposed to work on it together. But if I went upstairs, all I would think about was Pudding and her hair. Or, her no-hair.

"Hey, you're not watching!" said Andrew a little while later.

For the third time, the ball sailed right past my head.

"I guess I do not feel like playing anymore," I said.

I had to decide what to say to Natalie. Maybe I could tell her that Pudding had wandered into the catchy ward without permission. I could say, "Pudding caught a disease that made all her hair fall out. I'm terribly sorry."

I thought and thought about what to tell Natalie. Finally I saw Mommy's car pulling into the driveway. I ran to meet her.

"How is Mr. Kelly?" I asked.

"He looks quite well. And he loved his surprise visitors. He said to tell you he will be sure to return them as soon as he is out of the hospital," said Mommy.

I was very happy to hear that Mr. Kelly was better. I hoped I would see him soon. However, I did *not* want to see Natalie soon. But I knew she would arrive any minute. It was almost noon.

"Are you all right, Karen?" asked Mommy. "You look pale."

"I'm okay," I replied.

I did not want to tell Mommy or Seth about Pudding. If I did, I would have to tell them that I had played with Pudding's hair after Natalie told me not to.

I sat outside practicing my speech for Natalie. When her mother dropped her off, I was all ready.

"Hi, Karen!" called Natalie.

"Hi," I said. "Um, Natalie, I am very, very sorry. But I did not listen to you. I played with Pudding's hair and something happened. You'd better come see."

- I led Natalie up to my room. I went to the closet where I had hidden Pudding. I did not see her right away. I moved some shoes. I still did not see her. I moved some toys. I *still* did not see her. I looked in the closet for a long time.

"Where is Pudding?" asked Natalie when I came out.

"She was supposed to be in this closet," I replied. "I put her in here last night."

Natalie set her hands on her hips and shouted, "I WANT MY DOLL!"

"Well, I am sorry," I said. "I just cannot keep track of so many patients."

I swept my arm around, pointing to the many patients in my doll hospital. Even though some had gone to visit Mr. Kelly, there were still plenty of dolls all over the room.

"I am calling my mother to come pick me up," said Natalie. "You better find Pudding. I am not talking to you until you do, Karen Brewer!"

Natalie went downstairs to wait for her mommy. I went back to my closet to search for Pudding. I could not find her. I could not find her anywhere in my room.

Maybe Pudding was embarrassed about her bald head. Maybe she was hiding. I knew I would find Pudding. She had to be *somewhere*.

But what was I going to do about Natalie? How could we work on our May Day project if we were not talking?

Now, where would I hide if I were a doll?

The Good News

I looked for Pudding all over the hospital. Then I went back to my closet. I emptied out *everything*.

When I still could not find Pudding, I knew I would have to tell Mommy the truth. (I had told Mommy that Natalie went home because she did not feel well. Natalie really did look kind of sick after she found out what I had done to her doll.)

I went downstairs. Mommy was reading in the living room.

"Mommy, I have to tell you the real

reason Natalie went home," I began. I told her the whole story. I told her how I had pulled out Pudding's hair and then lost her.

"Maybe you gave Pudding to Mr. Kelly," said Mommy.

"No, I didn't. I mean, I do not think I did," I said. "But wherever she is, she is ruined. And Natalie will not talk to me. And if she will not talk to me, we cannot do our research project together."

"Karen, if you lost Natalie's doll, you will have to buy her a new one," said Mommy.

"A new doll? I cannot buy her a new doll. I just helped Natalie buy things to make the Maypole. And I need the money that's left over to buy a new dress for Hyacynthia. I promised to get her one when she was better."

"I am sure you have enough money to buy Natalie a doll. Hannie and Nancy paid for Hyacynthia's repairs, remember?" said Mommy. "And a new doll for Natalie is more important right now than a new dress for Hyacynthia. Don't you think so?"

"Yes," I said grumpily.

This was not a good day. Pudding was gone. Natalie was mad at me. I could not work on my research project. And now Hyacynthia could not get a new dress. Bullfrogs.

Ring! Ring! Mommy answered the phone. I hoped it was not more bad news.

It was not! It was good news! It was Mr. Kelly.

"Hello, Mr. Kelly," I said. "How are you feeling? When are you coming home?"

Mr. Kelly said he was coming home on Monday. He said he would love for me to visit him very soon.

"I'll ask Mommy," I replied.

Mommy said she would drive me to his house after school the next week. Mr. Kelly promised to give me back my dolls and animals then.

"I am so glad you are coming home, Mr. Kelly," I said. "I am so glad you are better. I will see you next week."

I was going to visit Mr. Kelly. Hurray!

The Surprise

After school on Wednesday, Mommy drove Andrew and me to Mr. Kelly's house. It was raining pretty hard. We splashed up the steps in our slickers and boots. I rang Mr. Kelly's bell.

Ding-ing-ing-ing. Dong-ong-ong-ong.

Mr. Kelly must have been sitting downstairs. He came to the door right away.

"Mr. Kelly!" I cried when I saw him. "You look good-as-new!"

"Thank you, Karen. I am so happy to see

you," said Mr. Kelly. "Come in, everyone. Come in out of that rain."

Mr. Kelly looked like he had lost a little weight at the hospital. But I could fix that. I gave him the package of oatmeal cookies Mommy and I made.

"They are a special healthy kind. They are good for your heart," I explained.

"I feel better already," said Mr. Kelly. "Please, hang your things over there and come sit down."

We had juice and oatmeal cookies while Mr. Kelly told us about his stay in the hospital.

"The nurses and the doctors were very nice to me," said Mr. Kelly. "But they like to wake you up at night to see how you are doing. And the food was not very good. There was nothing as delicious as these cookies."

"You would have liked my doll hospital better," I said.

"I'm sure you are right," said Mr. Kelly. "Oh, that reminds me. I want to return your dolls and animals. They were very good company."

Mr. Kelly got the bag from the closet.

"You might want to look inside, Karen," said Mr. Kelly.

"Oh, no. I do not have to count them," I said. "I trust you."

"Why don't you take a look anyway," said Mr. Kelly.

I could not figure out why Mr. Kelly wanted me to look inside. Until I opened the bag.

"Mr. Kelly, thank you!" I cried. "Look, Mommy! Look, Andrew!"

Mr. Kelly had fixed all my broken-down dolls and animals. They were sewed and repaired, with fresh paint on their faces. I was so surprised. And at the bottom of the bag was the best surprise of all.

"Pudding!" I shouted. "How did you get in there?"

"That's wonderful, Karen," said Mommy. "Now you do not need to buy Natalie another doll."

"And her hair has grown back," said Andrew. "I'm glad. She looked funny bald."

I was so excited about seeing Pudding again, I did not even notice her hair.

"Your Baby Grow-My-Hair will work like new now," said Mr. Kelly.

"Thank you, thank you, thank you!" I cried.

"You're very welcome, Karen," said Mr. Kelly.

"Will you still come to dinner at our house?" I asked.

"As soon as I am ready to go out, we will make a date," said Mr. Kelly.

When I returned to the little house, I called Natalie.

"Guess what!" I said. "I found Pudding. Her arm is fixed and her hair is just the way it was when you gave her to me. I will bring her to school for you tomorrow."

"Um, that's good news. Thank you, Karen," said Natalie.

Natalie sounded awfully quiet. I had thought she would be more excited to hear the good news about Pudding.

Oh, well, I thought. Maybe she needs time to stop being mad. She will be happy tomorrow when she sees how great Pudding looks.

Tomorrow. The next day was Thursday. My written report was due. I had been so busy worrying about Pudding that I had not finished writing it. I had one more page to go.

I took out a clean sheet of paper. At the very top, in my best handwriting I wrote, *Maypole*.

18

The Lost Maypole

Boo. It was raining again Thursday morning.

I had to put Pudding way down in my knapsack where she would not get wet. I did not want her to be a soggy mess with frizzy hair when Natalie saw her.

"Here you go, Pudding," I said, when we got to school. "You sit in Natalie's chair. She will be here very soon. And she will have our Maypole with her. I know you will like that."

Ms. Colman wanted us to bring in everything we were working on. She wanted to
see it all before we made our presentations
the next day.

In a few minutes, Natalie walked in. She
was carrying her notebook, her lunch, and
a dripping umbrella. But that was all. I did
not see the Maypole.

"Thank you for bringing Pudding," said
Natalie. She sat down at her desk and faced
the front of the room. She did not even look
at me.

"Where is it, Natalie? Where is the Maypole?" I asked.

"I don't have it," mumbled Natalie.

"What? Don't tell me you forgot it. I did
not forget to bring the report. Or Pudding,"
I said.

"I did not forget the Maypole," replied
Natalie. "It . . . it was thrown out."

"How could someone throw out our
beautiful Maypole?" I cried.

"I wrapped it up yesterday after school

because it was going to rain today. I didn't want the ribbons to get wet," explained Natalie.

"So?" I said.

"So I put it in the kitchen where I would remember to get it when I fixed my lunch this morning. But I guess I left it too close to the garbage. My daddy did not know what it was. He threw it out by accident," said Natalie in a choked up, teary voice.

Oh, *no*, I thought. This cannot be happening. Not to my first grown-up project.

"Now what are we going to do?" I moaned. "Ms. Colman expects a report *and* a Maypole."

"We will just have to tell her the truth," said Natalie.

"I guess so," I said. "Maybe she will give us some extra time. If we work really hard over the weekend, maybe we can make a new Maypole."

We ran to Ms. Colman as soon as she walked in. We told her what had happened to our Maypole.

"It was thrown out by accident. Things like that could happen to anyone. Even a grown-up. That is why they are called accidents," I explained.

"You are absolutely right, Karen," said Ms. Colman. "These things can happen to anyone."

We asked Ms. Colman if we could have more time.

"You may have until Monday," she replied.

The Maypole Dance

On Saturday morning, I woke up in my room at the big house.

"Good morning, Moosie. Do you want to hear a funny May Day rhyme?" I asked.

I made Moosie nod his head. Then I recited the rhyme I found in a book about May Day.

"Tomorrow's the fair, and I shall be there, stuffing my guts with gingerbread nuts."

Moosie and I laughed at the poem. Then I ate breakfast and Daddy drove me over to Natalie's house. We wanted to get started on our Maypole right away.

"Hi, Karen," said Natalie. "Come look. I have everything we need."

Natalie showed me a broom, ribbons, a box of gold foil, a hammer, and nails.

"How much did everything cost?" I asked. "I want to pay my share."

"Oh, no," replied Natalie. "Daddy wanted to pay for it because he threw out the other Maypole."

"But it was only an accident. So we should pay," I insisted. It seemed like the grown-up thing to do.

But Natalie would not take the money.

"Please tell your daddy thank you from me and Hyacynthia," I said. "This money will buy Hyacynthia her new dress."

We worked all morning long. Natalie's mommy helped us when we needed to use the hammer and nails.

When we had finished, our Maypole was beautiful! Three gold foil balls sat at the top. Eighteen colored ribbons hung down. That would be just the right number if everyone — even Ms. Colman — decided to join our May Day dance.

On Monday morning we arrived at school early.

"This Maypole was certainly worth waiting for, Karen and Natalie. It is beautiful," said Ms. Colman.

Yes! Natalie and I felt gigundoly proud of ourselves.

After attendance Ms. Colman announced, "We have two more presentations this morning. First we will hear from Hank and Bobby."

Hank had been absent on Friday. That is why he and Bobby were making their presentation today. They shuffled to the front of the room. They were dressed as two cardboard trees.

"Our holiday is Arbor Day," said Hank. "It is a day for planting trees in the spring."

They recited a poem called "Trees" by Joyce Kilmer. I could tell they were embarrassed. But I thought their presentation was very nice. Of course, it was not as nice as

92

our presentation was going to be. And we would give ours next.

"Psst! Natalie, your socks," I whispered.

Natalie bent down and pulled up her socks, while I began reading our report.

"May Day is a celebration of spring," I said. I told the class about Flora, the goddess of flowers. I told them about May baskets and May parties.

"And people of the villages gathered together and danced around a beautiful Maypole, just like this one." I said. "Who would like to come up and dance with us?"

"There are ribbons for everyone," added Natalie.

No one went to the front of the room. I could not believe it. I would have danced if someone had invited *me*. I gave Hannie and Nancy a Three Musketeers *you promised* look. It worked!

Hannie, Nancy, Natalie, and I each held onto the end of a ribbon. Then we danced around and around. We weaved our ribbons in and out, wrapping them around the pole.

While we were dancing, Natalie and I sang a spring song. *"Oh, the green grass grows all around, all around. The green grass grows all around!"*

You know what happened next? The rest of our classmates started singing with us. They sang as we danced around our Maypole. I felt as if we were back in olden times.

When we finished, the class clapped and clapped. And Ms. Colman gave us an A −.

Now that is a grown-up grade.

The Doll Wizard

"Attention, all dolls!" I said to my doll hospital. "I, Karen Brewer, got an A minus on my May Day research project."

The dolls clapped loudly.

I had already told everyone at the little house my news. And at the big house. I had called Mr. Kelly, too.

"That is wonderful news, Karen," he said. "On your next visit, will you show me your May Day dance?"

"Yes," I said. "I will even bring the Maypole."

We made our date for Thursday. Mommy drove me over to Mr. Kelly's house. This is who went with me: Andrew, Hannie, Nancy, Natalie (I wanted her to meet the person who had fixed Pudding), and Hyacynthia (I wanted Mr. Kelly to see how well his former patient was doing).

Ding-ing-ing-ing. Dong-ong-ong-ong.

We waited for Mr. Kelly to come downstairs. He was feeling much better and was working on the toys and dolls all day.

"Welcome, everyone," said Mr. Kelly when he opened the door.

I introduced Natalie. Then after everyone said hello, we went inside and did our Maypole dance. (Andrew held the pole.)

"Bravo! Bravo!" cried Mr. Kelly, when we had finished. "And now would you like to give Natalie your tour?"

"Yes, Natalie, come on," I said.

I showed her Mr. Kelly's repair shop and the doll hospital where he had fixed Pudding. She was impressed, just like everyone else.

After the tour, we went downstairs for juice and cookies.

"You know what, Mr. Kelly," I said. "Ms. Colman gave us a new assignment. We have to write a report *independently*. That means we do it by ourselves. It's all very grown-up."

"Yes, I see," said Mr. Kelly. "What do you have to write about?"

"We have to write about someone important in our lives. And guess who I picked? You!" I said.

"I am very honored," said Mr. Kelly. "I hope I am worthy of a whole report."

"Oh, you are!" I exclaimed. "I am going to interview you. I will write about your repair shop and all the dolls you have saved in your doll hospital."

"I will be happy to help in any way I can," replied Mr. Kelly.

"I already thought of a title for my report. I am going to call it *The Doll Wizard*," I said.

Mr. Kelly looked very happy. His eyes began to twinkle.

"Come, everyone. We have had a nice long visit. It's time to let Mr. Kelly get back to work," said Mommy.

Mr. Kelly walked us to the door.

"I think my dolls are all well now," I said. "They are going to go back to school in Nancy's room."

"You have made your dolls feel better, Karen. And you have made me feel better, too," said Mr. Kelly.

"I guess one doll wizard in Stoneybrook is plenty. But if you ever need an assistant wizard, call me, okay?" I asked.

"I sure will," replied Mr. Kelly.

Karen Brewer, Assistant Doll Wizard. That would be neat.

But for now I was Karen Brewer, writer of an independent school report. How grown-up could you get?

I hurried down the steps and hopped into Mommy's car. I waved to Mr. Kelly as we drove away.

"See you soon, Doll Wizard," I said. "See you soon."

About the Author

ANN M. MARTIN lives in New York City and loves animals, especially cats. She has two cats of her own, Mouse and Rosie.

Other books by Ann M. Martin that you might enjoy are *Stage Fright; Me and Katie (the Pest)*; and the books in *The Baby-sitters Club* series.

Ann likes ice cream and *I Love Lucy*. And she has her own little sister, whose name is Jane.

Little Sister

Don't miss #36

KAREN'S NEW FRIEND

All afternoon I sat next to Addie and helped her. When she dropped her pencil, I picked it up. When she needed her eraser, I pulled it out of her tote bag. When Ms. Colman told us to write some numbers on a piece of paper, I checked Addie's work. When Ms. Colman told us to take our spelling books home, I said to Addie, "That is your *blue* book."

"I know," she replied.

"Here, I will get it for you."

"I can get it," said Addie.

But I reached into her bag first.

The bell rang then. School was over. "I enjoyed being your helper," I told Addie. "And I am looking forward to tomorrow." I paused. Then I added, "I am going to be your very best friend, Addie."

101

LITTLE 🍎 APPLE ®

B·A·B·Y·S·I·T·T·E·R·S

Little Sister ®

by Ann M. Martin, author of *The Baby-sitters Club* ®

☐	MQ44300-3 #1	Karen's Witch	$2.75
☐	MQ44259-7 #2	Karen's Roller Skates	$2.75
☐	MQ44299-7 #3	Karen's Worst Day	$2.75
☐	MQ44264-3 #4	Karen's Kittycat Club	$2.75
☐	MQ44258-9 #5	Karen's School Picture	$2.75
☐	MQ43651-1 #10	Karen's Grandmothers	$2.75
☐	MQ43650-3 #11	Karen's Prize	$2.75
☐	MQ43649-X #12	Karen's Ghost	$2.75
☐	MQ43648-1 #13	Karen's Surprise	$2.75
☐	MQ43646-5 #14	Karen's New Year	$2.75
☐	MQ43645-7 #15	Karen's in Love	$2.75
☐	MQ43644-9 #16	Karen's Goldfish	$2.75
☐	MQ43643-0 #17	Karen's Brothers	$2.75
☐	MQ43642-2 #18	Karen's Home-Run	$2.75
☐	MQ43641-4 #19	Karen's Good-Bye	$2.95
☐	MQ44823-4 #20	Karen's Carnival	$2.75
☐	MQ44824-2 #21	Karen's New Teacher	$2.95
☐	MQ44833-1 #22	Karen's Little Witch	$2.95
☐	MQ44832-3 #23	Karen's Doll	$2.95
☐	MQ44859-5 #24	Karen's School Trip	$2.75
☐	MQ44831-5 #25	Karen's Pen Pal	$2.75
☐	MQ44830-7 #26	Karen's Ducklings	$2.75
☐	MQ44829-3 #27	Karen's Big Joke	$2.75
☐	MQ44828-5 #28	Karen's Tea Party	$2.75
☐	MQ44825-0 #29	Karen's Cartwheel	$2.75
☐	MQ45645-8 #30	Karen's Kittens	$2.75
☐	MQ45646-6 #31	Karen's Bully	$2.95
☐	MQ45647-4 #32	Karen's Pumpkin Patch	$2.95
☐	MQ45648-2 #33	Karen's Secret	$2.95
☐	MQ45650-4 #34	Karen's Snow Day	$2.95
☐	MQ45652-0 #35	Karen's Doll Hosital	$2.95

Available wherever you buy books, or use this order form.

Scholastic Inc., P.O. Box 7502, 2931 E. McCarty Street, Jefferson City, MO 65102

Please send me the books I have checked above. I am enclosing $ _____
(please add $2.00 to cover shipping and handling). Send check or money order - no cash
or C.O.Ds please.

Name _____

Address_____

City_____State/Zip_____

Tell us your birth date! _____
Please allow four to six weeks for delivery. Offer good in U.S.A. only. Sorry, mail orders are not
available to residents to Canada. Prices subject to change.   BLS792

© 1992 Walt Disney Company.

It's a Super Special Month!

YOU CAN WIN A TRIP TO WALT DISNEY WORLD RESORT®!

Enter The Winter Super Special Giveaway for The Baby-sitters Club® and Baby-sitters Little Sister® fans!

Visit Walt Disney World Resort...and experience all the excitement of Peter Pan, Tinkerbell, and a whole cast of characters! We'll send the **Grand Prize Winner** of this Giveaway and his/her parent or guardian (age 21 or older) on an all-expense paid trip, for 5 days and 4 nights, to Walt Disney World Resort in Florida!

10 Second Prize Winners get a Baby-sitters Club Record Album!
25 Third Prize Winners get a Baby-sitters Club T-shirt!

Early Bird Bonus!
100 early entries will receive a Baby-sitters Club calendar! But hurry!
To qualify, your entry must be postmarked by December 1, 1992.

Just fill in the coupon below or write the information on a 3" x 5" piece of paper and mail to:
THE WINTER SUPER SPECIAL GIVEAWAY, P.O. Box 7500, Jefferson City, MO 65102.
Return by March 31, 1993.

Rules: Entries must be postmarked by March 31, 1993. Winners will be picked at random and notified by mail. No purchase necessary. Valid only in the U.S. Void where prohibited. Taxes on prizes are the responsibility of the winners and their immediate families. Employees of Scholastic Inc.; its agencies, affiliates, subsidiaries; and their immediate families are not eligible. For a complete list of winners, send a self-addressed stamped envelope after March 31, 1993 to: The Winter Super Special Giveaway Winners List, at the address provided above.

The Winter Super Special Giveaway

Name _____ Age _____

Street _____

City _____ State/Zip _____

Where did you buy this book?

☐ Bookstore   ☐ Drugstore   ☐ Supermarket   ☐ Library
☐ Book Club   ☐ Book Fair   ☐ Other_____ (specify)

BSC692

Pssst... Know what? You can find out **everything** there is to know about *The Baby-sitters Club*. Join the BABY-SITTERS FAN CLUB! Get the hot news on the series, the inside scoop on all the Baby-sitters, and lots of baby-sitting fun...just for $4.95!

With your **two-year** membership, you get:

    ☆ An official membership card!
    ☆ A colorful banner!
    ☆ The exclusive Baby-sitters Fan Club quarterly
      newsletter with baby-sitting tips, activities and more!

Just fill in the coupon below and mail with payment to:
THE BABY-SITTERS FAN CLUB,
Scholastic Inc., P.O. Box 7500, 2931 E. McCarty Street, Jefferson City, MO 65012.

The Baby-sitters Fan Club

❑ **YES!** Enroll me in The Baby-sitters Fan Club! I've enclosed my check or money order (no cash please) for $4.95 made payable to Scholastic Inc.

Name _____ Age _____

Street _____

City _____ State/Zip _____

Where did you buy this *Baby-sitters Club* book?

❑ Bookstore   ❑ Drugstore   ❑ Supermarket   ❑ Book Club
❑ Book Fair   ❑ Other_____(specify)
Not available outside of U.S. and Canada.

BSC791